Jodie Callaghan's story *The Train* was
the winner of The Mi'gmaq Writers Award
in 2010, an annual contest run by the
Mi'gmawei Mawiomi Secretariat of
Listuguj Mi'gmaq Nation to recognize
talented Mi'gmaq writers.

The Train

written by Jodie Callaghan

illustrated by Georgia Lesley

Second Story Press

Ashley was smaller than her sister, but old enough to walk herself to school every morning and back again at the end of the day.

She took her time when she walked—kicking dirt to uncover stones and pieces of colored glass, which she kept on the windowsill in her bedroom.

The sun was exceptionally bright this afternoon.
Ashley had to shield her eyes with a hand to see the road.

A car sped past her, billowing up a cloud of dirt.
It stung her eyes, and she stopped to wipe them.
Squinting, she followed the tire tracks up the road
to where the old train station used to stand.

A small figure stood in the tall grass by the tracks.

Ashley recognized the way the figure leaned against his cane. She smiled and broke into a run. The beads in her backpack jingled in their tin, and her schoolbooks bounced, heavy against her back.

"Uncle!" she shouted. "Uncle!"

Ashley's uncle turned and greeted her with a smile. "Hello, tu's," he said, extending his good arm to give her a hug. She rushed into him, burrowing her face in his wool jacket. He was warm against her cheek. She inhaled deeply. He smelled like sage. She pulled away and looked up at him.

"Uncle, what are you doing here?"

The corners of his eyes crinkled, and one side of his mouth turned up in a lopsided smile as Ashley's uncle looked at her, but she could see the light in his eyes. He focused his gaze down the train tracks. The planks of wood between the metal rails were rotting and broken from years and years of weather damage. It was easy to see the community no longer thought of this place.

"I'm waiting for the train," he let out in a small voice.

Ashley looked down the track too. It was worn and overgrown with weeds—no longer fit for a train. She giggled. "Uncle! The train doesn't come here anymore."

"I know, tu's." He shifted his weight onto his cane. His smile drooped slowly. "I know."

Ashley stopped smiling as well and
furrowed her brow in concern.
"What's wrong? Why are you so sad?"

A look of indecision crossed his face as he glanced down at his small niece. "Come here," he said.

Uncle hobbled over to a piece of concrete foundation left from the old train station. He sat down and balanced his cane atop his knees. Ashley followed, sitting in the tall grass by his feet.

She plucked a dandelion and rubbed it against the back of her hand, tracing a heart with the yellow stain.

"I'm sad because our people have forgotten about this place," her uncle said, looking off down the track.

Ashley almost turned to see what he was looking at, but she knew nothing was there. She had walked by this place a thousand times. She focused on her uncle, studying the lines on his small face. Wisps of gray hair fluttered around his head as the wind blew from behind him, yet he looked young to her right now.

"What happened?" she wondered aloud.

"This place is very important to me, and to people like me," he said proudly.

"Why?" she asked. What could be so important about a weeded-over train track?

Uncle clutched his cane in both hands and planted the rubber end firmly on the ground. He leaned into it, looking at where she sat in the tall grass.

"A long time ago, there was a train that ran through this place," he began. "It would come maybe once a month to drop things off, things like rice and potatoes—stuff from outside of the reserve." He took his handkerchief out of his pocket and placed it on his lap, picking at loose threads as he spoke. "Giju' would send me and your Grandfather Timmy down to meet the train because we were the oldest. We would all line up here to wait with our baskets, and after we got our rations, we would walk home. Timmy and I would always sneak a potato each to eat on the way. We ate them raw, like they were apples!"

Ashley giggled at the thought of Grandfather Timmy and Uncle as small boys, eating raw potatoes.

Her uncle continued.

"One day, Giju' sent the four oldest kids out with baskets. It was early fall, but she made us take our winter coats. She was crying, and we didn't know why. Giju' didn't cry often, but when she got started, she couldn't stop. She gave us each a kiss and sent us to the train station." He looked down at the foundation he was sitting on. "When we arrived, there were children from all over the village. I saw my cousin Benny, so I asked him what was going on. He didn't know." Uncle pointed to the broken track. "The train was already here. A few men were standing by the open cargo doors. They pointed at us and said, 'Okay, you first.' And then they put us on the train."

Ashley wanted to speak, but her uncle's expression stopped her. He began again.

"My brother and sister were a bit younger than me, so they got put on a different car. Timmy and I were bigger, and they moved us to the front. When we got to the school, the nuns told us to get inside. They took our clothes. They took our baskets. They cut off all of our hair. They told us we were no longer native. And if we put up a fuss, we were hit, sometimes worse...." His voice trailed off into a whisper. "We weren't allowed to speak our language. We weren't allowed to be Nnu."

Ashley's uncle picked up his handkerchief and blew his nose. He clutched it tightly in his right hand, his shoulders trembling softly.

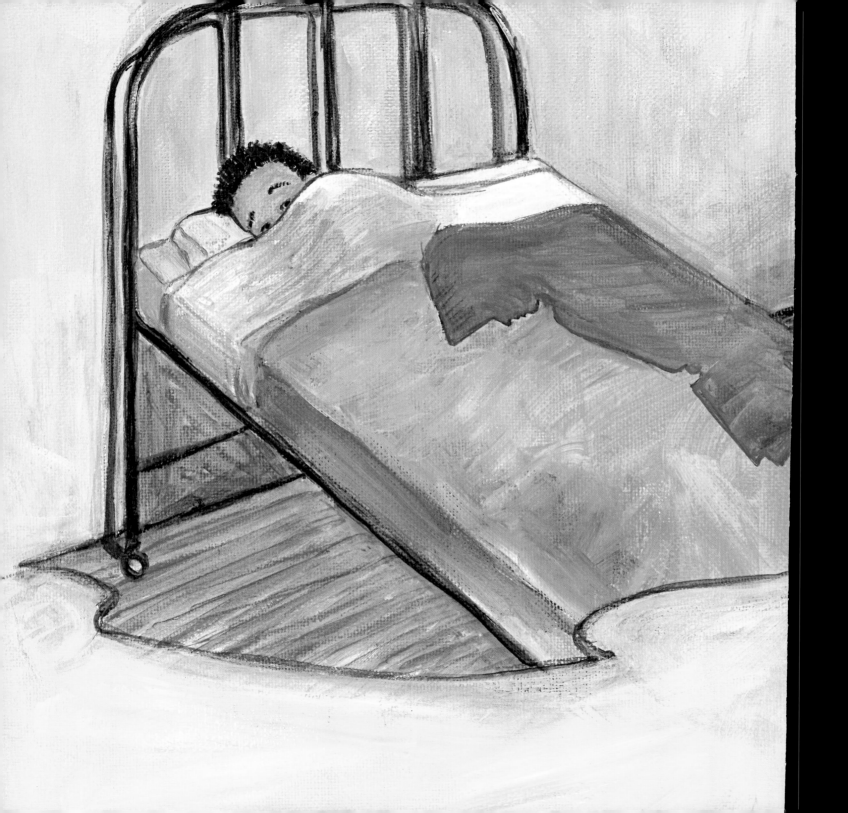

"I was there for six years," he told his niece. "I didn't know how to speak any English, so I didn't talk to many people. I was like a little mouse, hiding in my room." He smiled softly, tears gathering in the corners of his eyes. "I tried to be invisible. But they found me."

Ashley stared down at the grass. She plucked a few pieces and tied them into knots. "Why did they do that?" She looked up. The deep lines in her uncle's face had softened. His eyes glittered as the sun shone down on his brown skin.

"Because we were different," he said calmly.

Ashley's cheeks grew warmer. She felt angry and confused. "Why didn't your mommy and daddy come and get you? Why didn't they stop the train?" She felt her own tears welling up.

Her uncle shrugged. "They didn't know. No one knew. But that train changed everything."

"Were you sad to leave?" Ashley asked.

He nodded, and his voice began to tremble again. "There was nobody beside us waving good-bye. There was nobody there to hug us and to kiss us. Or to remember who we were when we left that day."

"I'm sorry, Uncle," Ashley choked through her tears.

He placed his good hand on her shoulder. "It's not your fault, tu's."

He lifted her chin and smiled at her. "You and your sister make me so happy. When I hear you laugh and see you run and play, it makes me think that one day, everything will be okay again. One day, we won't be so sad." He paused and looked toward the track for a moment. "I wanted you to know where your family has come from, Ashley. So you can be proud of where you are going."

Ashley wiped her tears with her sleeve. "Is that why you come to sit here, Uncle? To remember what happened?"

He nodded and thought for a moment. "I come here to remember what happened, but I also come here to wait."

"What are you waiting for?" she asked, craning her neck to look at the tracks, broken and rusted, still in the evening light, just how she had left them.

"I'm waiting for what we lost that day to come back to us," he said.

"Why?" she asked.

"Because if I don't, who will?" he asked, closing his eyes tightly.

Ashley reached up and touched Uncle's fingers. They uncurled and her hand rested, small, inside his. He looked at his little niece. She smiled up at him and said, "Don't worry, Uncle. I will wait with you."

Glossary of Mi'gmaq Words

tu's   Short for ntus, which means "my daughter."
It's used for young girls as a term of endearment.

Giju'   Mother.

Nnu   Indigenous person.

It is estimated that over 150,000 Indigenous children in Canada were sent to residential schools where they were forced to live away from their families and their communities. While at the schools, the children were often mistreated and weren't allowed to speak their native languages or practice their traditions. These children were survivors.

For my grams,
I love you and I miss you.
—Jodie Lynn

———————————

Library and Archives Canada Cataloguing in Publication

Title: The train / written by Jodie Callaghan ; illustrated by Georgia Lesley.
Names: Callaghan, Jodie, 1984- author. | Lesley, Georgia, illustrator.
Identifiers: Canadiana 20190187328 | ISBN 9781772601299 (hardcover)
Subjects: CSH: Native peoples—Canada—Residential schools—Juvenile fiction. | LCGFT: Picture books.
Classification: LCC PS8605.A4594 T73 2020 | DDC jC813/.6—dc23

Printed and bound in China

Second Story Press gratefully acknowledges the support of the Ontario Arts Council
and the Canada Council for the Arts for our publishing program. We acknowledge the
financial support of the Government of Canada through the Canada Book Fund.

ONTARIO ARTS COUNCIL
CONSEIL DES ARTS DE L'ONTARIO
an Ontario government agency
un organisme du gouvernement de l'Ontario

Canada Council   Conseil des Arts
for the Arts   du Canada

Funded by the Government of Canada
Financé par le gouvernement du Canada   Canada

Published by
Second Story Press
20 Maud Street, Suite 401
Toronto, Ontario, Canada
M5V 2M5
www.secondstorypress.ca